# ASLEEP IN A HEAP

Library of Congress Cataloging-in-Publication Data

Winthrop, Elizabeth.

Asleep in a heap / Elizabeth Winthrop ; illustrated by Mary Morgan.

p.   cm.

Summary: A little girl finds so many things to do before she is
ready for bed that she is the last of her family to fall asleep.

ISBN 0-8234-0992-9

[1. Bedtime — Fiction.]   I. Morgan, Mary, 1957–     ill.   II. Title.

PZ7.W768As   1993

[E] — dc20      92-11310      CIP      AC

# ASLEEP IN A HEAP

## by Elizabeth Winthrop

## illustrated by Mary Morgan

Holiday House/New York

"Julia," called Mama. "It's bedtime."
"Julia," called Daddy, "where are you?"
"Julia, it's time for B-E-D,"
 called Molly, her older sister.
 Julia was playing in her room.
 She did not answer
 because she did not want to go to bed.
 She was too busy.

First she drew some pictures.

Then she dressed her dolls
for their evening walk.

Then she sang a little song
and danced a little dance.

"Julia," called Mama again.
Julia pulled her blanket over her head.
She was sure nobody could see her.
She sat very still
and waited for her mother to go away.

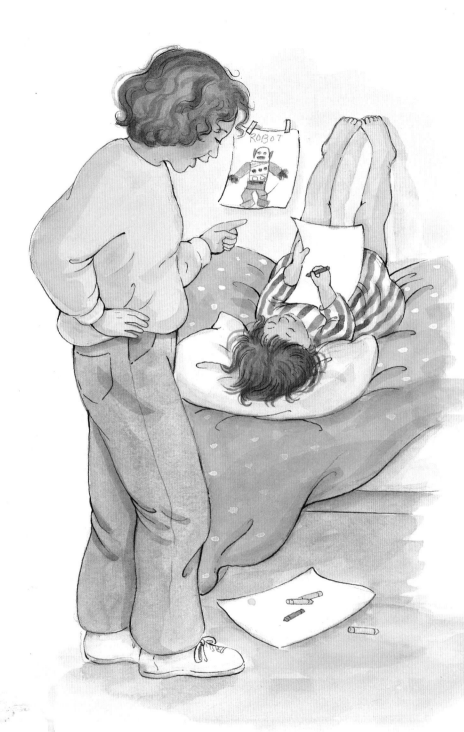

"Julia," said her mother. "It's bedtime."

"I'm not here," said Julia. "I'm busy."

"You can finish your pictures tomorrow," Mama said.

"I have to finish them tonight," said Julia. "And then I have many other very important things to do. They will take a very long time."

"They will take no more than ten minutes," Mama said. "Because then it's bedtime."

Julia finished her pictures.
She tacked them up on her bulletin board.
Then she put her dolls, Katie and Sarah,
in the baby carriage.

She pushed the baby carriage out the back
door and around the house.
"Julia," called Daddy.
"Come in now, it's time for bed."
"I'm busy," said Julia, and she pushed faster
and faster.

The dolls bumped up and down in the carriage.
Katie almost fell out.
Sarah looked sick to her stomach.
Julia was hot and sweaty.
She had mud on the hem of her nightgown
and mud on the bottom of her feet.

"Julia, you're a mess," said Daddy.
"Now you need another bath."
He took Julia by the hand and led
her into the bathroom.
He ran the water into the tub.
Julia poured in the soap bubbles.

Then she hopped in.

Her father lay down on the floor.

"You look very tired, Daddy," said Julia.

"I will sing you a going-to-sleep song."

"Mmm," said her father. "That's nice."

Julia looked over the edge of the bathtub.

"Are you asleep, Daddy?"

"Noooo," said her father in a slow, sleepy voice.

"That's good," Julia said. "Because I haven't
started singing yet."

"I know," said her father. "I'm listening."

Julia sang a song about bubbles in the sky.

She made it up as she went along.

When she stopped singing,
it was very quiet in the bathroom.

Her father had fallen asleep.

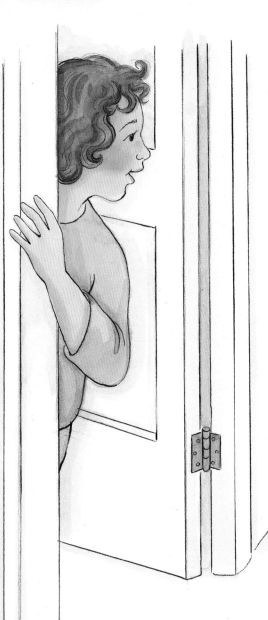

Her mother opened the door.

"Daddy was very tired," said Julia.

"I sang him a song, and he fell asleep."

"I know how Daddy feels," said Mama.

"Time to get out of the bath. It's getting late."

"No," said Julia. "I'm very busy with my bubbles."

"Julia," said Mama in a stern voice.

"Just ten more minutes," said Julia.

"Five," said Mama. "I will pull the plug
and when the water's all gone, it's time
to go to bed."

"I will sing you my going-to-sleep song," said Julia.
"All right," said Mama.
　She lay down with her head on Daddy's stomach.

Molly stuck her head in the door.
"Isn't Julia asleep yet?" she asked.
"No, but Daddy is," said Mama.
"Julia's singing me a song."

"I want to lie down too," said Molly.
  She put her head on her mother's stomach.
"This is comfy," said Molly,
"except your stomach makes funny little noises."
"Daddy's does too," said Mama.

"Quiet, everybody," said Julia.
"I will sing you my song.
   Then you won't hear the funny noises."
   So Julia sang her song about the bubbles in the sky
   and the birds that chased them
   and the wind that blew them away.
   When the water had all gone down the drain,
   Julia stopped singing.

She peeked over the edge of the bathtub.
Now her mother and Molly were both asleep.
Her whole family was asleep,
asleep in a heap on the bathroom floor.

Julia stood up.
She dried herself off with a towel
   and put on her clean nightgown.
         She put her ear down
            next to Molly's stomach.
            It made funny little noises too
            and it was very soft.
         "Maybe I will take a nap,"
         Julia said to herself.
         "Just a very short nap
            before I put my dolls to bed
            and dance my little dance."

So she lay down
with her head on Molly's soft stomach.
She listened to the funny little noises.
"This is comfy," whispered Julia.
"Very comfy."
Soon she was asleep too.
Fast asleep on the top of the heap.